# Hell is For Mailmen

## A Novella

# Chris Griffy

# One: A New Career

I don't know which I found more surprising about the afterlife; that it had a mailman, or that I was it.

At least, I *think* this is the afterlife. I remember pain. And darkness. I don't remember dying, or any circumstance I was in that might have caused death. I didn't see any bright lights or my family beckoning me. But would I? The only accounts of the mechanics of death we have are from people who haven't actually died, so one could be forgiven in labeling their testimony unreliable at best.

It could be the apocalypse, but it's a damn weird one. No destruction of property, no bodies, no zombies, no fallout and, most importantly, no people. No animals. None.

Except me.

All I can truly go with is the facts I have. I woke up in a one-bedroom house, moderately but sufficiently furnished. A few chairs, though why more than one when I couldn't entertain, I don't know. A couch; a small kitchen with refrigerator and pantry, always fully, if not appealingly, stocked; stove; microwave; coffee maker (this is how I know I'm not in Hell. In Hell, there wouldn't be coffee). There were a dozen or so books, apparently randomly selected. *The Maltese Falcon*, *Alice in Wonderland*, and *Brief History of Time* exist companionably together on the same shelf. I'd have expected a Bible, or *Paradise Lost*, but apparently whoever or whatever runs this place doesn't seem to be fond of religious literature. Pity. Clues would have been helpful. There's also a rather comfortable full bed. You wouldn't think the dead (undead?) would sleep, but they do. Well, I do. I don't have any other undead/apocalypse survivor/unraptured people to compare notes with.

And, the most important features (besides the coffee pot); a hook beside the door to hang a bag full of mail and a hipster-approved fixed gear bicycle, complete with saddlebag connectors, outside the door. The tools of what I discovered were my newly assigned trade.

After the initial confusion wore off and I got used to the

house, I set out to explore my new neighborhood. It's your stock straight out of the '50s ready-made slice of suburbia, filled with rows of Malvina Reynolds' "Little Boxes." There was immaculate landscaping, despite never being tended that I could see. But no stores and, again, no people. Best I could tell, I had the joint to myself.

You never realize how *loud* Earth is. What you previously called silent is in truth a cacophony of sounds. The hum of a central air unit (despite having no noticeable climate control mechanism, my home stayed a comfortable 68 degrees). The buzz of insects. The subtle rustle of leaves as small creatures scurry from your presence. An airplane passing high over. None of those register as "noise" when they're always there. But when you don't have them the silence is truly complete. The slap of your feet on pavement sounds like gunshots. The hum of bicycle tires like an engine. I found a pack of playing cards, the only thing beside the books meant for entertainment, and put the jokers in my bicycle spokes like a kid, just to have some noise.

You also don't realize how *dark* Earth is without electricity. My home appeared to be the only one on the grid. There are no street lights, no glow of televisions from house windows, no car headlights. There's a moon, but it never seems to cycle, remaining permanently at a barely lit crescent. There are stars but no constellations that I can identify. "Night" is odd here. I'd lay out in a green and empty patch of land I thought of as the "park" at night and stare up at the heavens, or down from the heavens, or from whatever direction someone here looks to the heavens. The complete darkness make even the crescent moon shine like a beacon. I've never really been an astronomy buff, that I can remember, but the lack of standard forms of entertainment makes hobbies from what is available.

One thing I missed on my initial tour of the houses were the letter slots. At the time I didn't realize how much of my "life" would be dictated by these tiny holes in nondescript doors; how much of my day spent delivering letters to empty houses, presumably to pile on the other side of the door, unread by human eyes. At least I never saw any. Or heard any. The letters had no names. Just a street address, adding further to the confusion over whether I even delivered to anyone.

I knew I was a mailman almost instantly upon returning to my home and seeing the bag on the hook. I'd never been a mailman. I was, once, a professor of Medieval Studies at a college private enough to have a degree in medieval studies for trust fund babies who would never need their college degree to find a career. I wouldn't have recognized the bag when alive. But here I instantly knew what it was, knew how to sort mail, knew how to hook it onto my bicycle, and had a near total compulsion to deliver. There was even a uniform. I would like to have refused to put it on, but it was all my closet held. It was either wear the uniform or deliver the mail starkers. Not that there were any cops to issue nude bicycle riding citations.

After a first few days of pedaling around my "route" dutifully shoving mail into empty houses, I decided this was not what I wanted to do with my afterlife. So I did the only thing I could. I resisted. I've never been a very good conformist, even if some theoretical "god" might be the one demanding conformity.

So I began Operation Fuck You, God. It's a working title.

It wasn't a working strategy, though.

# Two: Hard Lessons Learned

Day 1 of the operation I refused to deliver the mail. I fought the increasing pull to do so with all my will, reading books, eating food, and generally trying to ignore the bag on the hook. I took a walk but the sight of the mail slots made the longing worse, so I jogged circles around my tiny back yard. I wished for a basketball hoop. Or a dog. I played solitaire with my lone deck of cards. I went to sleep proud I'd resisted. I could do this!

Day 2 found a second bag had joined the first, and the pull even stronger. I managed to ignore it, barely. I went to sleep that night proud again for sticking it to the man (or maybe the woman. I wasn't entirely sure of the sex, or even existence, of my Postmaster.)

Day 3 saw yet another bag and a kitchen devoid of food and running water. Within a few hours, an overwhelming hunger and thirst overcame me, a lot more than should be warranted for a single day. But then time is mercurial here, so who knows? It could have been a week, a month, a year, an hour, a second. My throat was parched, the hole in my stomach growling and rumbling in protest and occasionally tossing out a twinge of pain just to remind me it was not happy. At all.

I delivered the mail. All three bags. The daylight lasted until I finished, as it always did no matter when I began, twilight falling just as I arrived back at the house. When I returned home, the pantries were stocked and the water was on. I ate and drank like I was in a Caligulan orgy. Without the sex. Hard to have a true orgy when you're your only partner. I went to sleep with the satisfying stretched feeling of a post-Thanksgiving dinner coma. This should have taught me a lesson. But, despite a Doctoral education, I've never been accused of learning easily.

The next two days I delivered the mail without complaint. I was unsure if you could die of hunger or thirst here. I'd never hold out that long. I've never been good with pain. I kind always wanted a tattoo (the Book of Kells. Got to keep the Medieval Studies professor cred intact) but I'm afraid of pain. The hollow stomach and swollen tongue/dry mouth was all I could handle.

For my next act of defiance I burned the mail. The kitchen had matches. I don't know why as there was nothing to light. It could have been a pyrotechnic version of Eve's Apple. If so, I failed that test hard. I dumped the bag in the street, touched match to letters, and danced around the fire like a crazy man. I even tossed the bag in. It felt good. Like cleansing my responsibilities in fire. I didn't feel the compulsion to deliver that night, and I thought I'd won.

I woke screaming, my arms and legs searing as if I had been burned at the stake and cut down before I died. There wasn't a mark on me, but the pain made the hunger and thirst feel like a pricked finger. I moaned. I cried. I dragged myself into the kitchen to bathe my arms and legs in cold water that didn't help. I cursed every god I could think of, from Yahweh to Vishnu, just to cover all my bases. I felt like I was still being burned the rest of the day, enough that I finally took a knife from the drawer and tried to slit my own throat, but then my throat hurt too. No blood flowed, no cut appeared, and no death happened. It felt like a rug burn.

The burns stopped hurting the second I mounted my bicycle and delivered the bag of mail hanging innocently on its hook, though the pain at my throat remained for a few days, perhaps a final punishment to remind me. It was becoming apparent that, if I didn't deliver the mail, it was going to go badly for me. Also, there was nothing else to do. All twelve of the books had been read, a couple twice, and after the burning incident all the Jacks disappeared from my card deck, rendering solitaire an exercise in frustration. The mail route at least gave me a way to pass the time and, no matter when I went to bed after, I woke to a fresh morning and a fresh bag.

It took a week (month? Year?) before I tried any stunts again.

It wasn't stubbornness that got me. The burns didn't ever leave my mind. It was curiosity. I guess it didn't exactly kill the cat, since all evidence pointed to this particular cat joining the choir invisible some time ago. But it fucked me up.

Worse than the burns.

I read the mail.

Only a few letters. Who'd miss them when there was no one to deliver to? What was I delivering? Blank papers?

The type on the first was closely spaced, without paragraphs, commas, and not a ton of periods. I don't think if I'm in this place forever I'll be able to forget a word of it...

"Oh God, oh God, whatdidido? She'sgone, shewentiwentilost her imadeithappenicaused itall. Ifgodistherekillme, takemeholdme shelterforgiveredeemtakemeto HelltakemetoHeaventake metooblivion. Kill me."

The words went on for two pages, front and back, tightly spaced words coming in an increasingly desperate and insane flow, the spelling getting worse until at the end it was just lines of gibberish. He killed his lover, or hurt her, or left her harmed in some way. That part was clear. How it ended then was not. Suicide? Decades filled with that kind of monologue in his head? The not knowing was the worst part.

I thought. I opened another. It was less panicked, but so much worse in its calm. So much.

"This is best. Best for me. Best for everyone. To the ones I love, I'm sorry. I cause you pain to heal you. To those I hate, fuck you. I'll see you in Hell. To everyone else, you don't know me anyway. Not yet."

Another suicide? A murder? The passionless prose chilled me in a way the desperate missive didn't. That person was in the grip of insanity. This person; this person knew his (her?) mind. The actions were deliberate. The mind sane, or at least lucid. Which is so much worse.

And the last one. The one that stayed with me for weeks. The one that haunted my sleep.

"You should have done more."

One sentence. Floating in a vast sea of white. The other two were obviously the inner conflict of the man/woman involved. This... was it external? Was it from someone so dissociated he/she spoke in second person? Or, and this is the part that fucked me up, a pronouncement of judgment from the shadowy "God" I didn't really believe in.

No. No. The implications were horrifying. Is this what I do? Are there people in the houses after all? Am I their torturer, the demon who unknowingly taunts them with their own sins, stuffing their own confessions through a hole in their door? Do they fear me, cower from me, believe me a part of a divine punishment I never agreed to inflict? Are they right?

This last part hurts most. Maybe I'm the bogeyman for hundreds of souls, the one whose arrival they dread, whose visage they fear so much they never look. Maybe Hell is a mail route. And I'm a demon in a postman's uniform.

You'd think this sobering realization would be enough punishment to satisfy my Cosmic Postmaster. I went to bed humbled and troubled, though sleep took me immediately. It always did.

The next morning I woke to no mailbag on the hook. Just a single letter resting on my chest.

Addressed to me.

I didn't read the letter. Maybe it contained an explanation. Maybe it contained instructions. Maybe it even contained a written warning from my "boss." It could, considering the lack of mail, have even contained a letter of termination. This would have worried me at another time. What am I if fired as a mailman in a place that appears to need nothing but a mailman? But it only fleetingly crossed my mind.

Instead the letter, my name and address in the block print I'd come to call "God Font," looking just like the tortured, confessional letters I delivered daily. The only letter I'd ever seen with a name. At that moment I didn't care what instructions, explanations, warnings, or even an unlikely Employee of the Month Award (though, as the only employee, I seemed a shoe in) it contained. What it possibly could be was too horrific.

I burned the letter.

I winced when doing so, remembering the punishment for burning the mail. But at that moment I didn't care. I'd take the searing pain over the psychological damage of that envelope's potential. That letter, with nowhere to be delivered, taunting me from inside my home for eternity. My Monkey's

Paw.

I went to bed wondering what torture the next morning would bring, but profoundly happy the letter was ash, kicked and scattered so it no longer resembled paper.

I woke up with no pain. Just a mailbag on a hook and the familiar longing. I delivered the mail, mechanically sorting and shoving through letter slots, barely remembering until it was done.

# Three: Pages And Memory

That night the notebook was lying at my bedside, a pencil on top. That night I began to write down my memories.

I remembered only parts of my life. Increasingly less as "time" went on. I remembered my best friend in 4th grade. His name was Peter and he had the thickest glasses I ever saw. But my profession, Medieval Studies. That I questioned. Was it Medieval Literature? History? Middle English? Chaucer seemed familiar to me. So did King Arthur. Were they medieval or some other period? I didn't remember and didn't think I ever would again. What else had I lost? What else of me was no longer of anyone? What happened when I forgot it all?

That night I began writing, the words coming out like oil from a well. Everything I was, what I remember of it, before today was summed up in those pages, written with a pencil that never required sharpening, in a notebook that never ran out of paper. I knew this as surely as I knew how to sort, how to plot a route, how to deliver mail. I wondered if one day I'd even forget the notebook existed, forget that I could flip through its pages and remember some of the past, truly forget everything. Be nothing but a Clockwork Mailman, with no recollection I was anything else. The routine my existence; the mail my world.

The mail was the one constant in this purgatory/apocalypse. It was the thing I most wanted to forget and the thing I never could. Every morning the bag hangs on the hook. Every morning I sorted the mail, loaded the saddlebags onto the bicycle, and pedaled down the streets shoving mail into small slots in doors to homes that, by all available evidence, stood quiet as tombs. Except King Tut didn't receive letters. That I know. I'm not even sure of the significance of that name. It's there, but not *truly* there.

I wished I had a radio. An mp3 player and the collected works of Pink Floyd (Pink? Floyd Cramer? Are these people members of the same band or altogether different?) would be better. I wasn't bored, exactly. Once I began delivering the mail, a kind of trance came over me, my world reduced to the hum of tires, the clack-clack of playing cards in bicycle spokes, the paper on metal rasp of letters shoved through slots. I didn't hurry, or tarry. It wouldn't have mattered if I did. Whether I started at the crack of dawn or lounged around the house all day before mounting my bicycle, the sun always set just as I pulled onto my street at the end of delivery. So long as I didn't go to bed, the day seemed content that I intended to perform my duties and paused for me to do so in my own time.

The period between deliveries was mine. If I felt like it, I could fall into bed as soon as my delivery was over and wake from a dreamless sleep to light and a mailbag. But that seemed a horrifying prospect. Like I had officially given up on "living", whatever living meant here. So I kept myself busy reading, jogging around the block, playing solitaire (once I got back with the program, my Jacks reappeared a few days later), writing in my journal, eating.

The Cosmic Grocers of this place leave quite a lot to be desired. There was some basic variety. Some staple fruit and vegetables. Occasionally a hunk of meat. But the one thing that never changed was a freezer chock full of Hungry Man Salisbury Steak dinners. I don't know why. Maybe the Cosmic Costco had a sale. But I got so sick of Hungry Man Salisbury Steak, mashed potatoes, and gravy ("with brownie dessert!" the packaging exclaimed, as if a bit of half-cooked chocolate bread, doughy in the center, tooth-breakingly hard at the edges, would make it all better). I tore a page from my journal, wrote "Could you please knock it off with the Hungry Man Salisbury Steak? Some variety would be appreciated, please!" and stuck it inside the freezer. Since I never saw or heard anyone come into my house, I don't know if there was anyone to read the note, but it seemed worth the chance.

The next day the note was gone, as were all of the Hungry Man Salisbury Steaks; all replaced by row upon row of Hungry Man Pot Roast Dinner (with apple crumble dessert!). The first couple of days were happy ones. Anything not Salisbury Steak was welcome. That soon changed. I had already begun to wonder if I weren't in purgatory but in some kind of giant social experiment, or a some kind of voyeuristic television program. All I knew for sure was I came to fucking hate Hungry Man Pot Roast. But, under the supposition of the devil you know, I did not taunt my Cosmic Grocer with more requests. A week later, my refrigerator had a massive (and, to my shock, very much alive) king crab in it. It was the first living thing I'd seen since getting here. If I'd had a tank, I might have saved it. Eating it seemed wrong, somehow, when it was my only companion in life. I might have tried even without the tank. Who knows what kind of strange physics work here?

Then I thought of another night of Hungry Man Pot Roast.

The next morning I was once again the only living thing in this place.

For variety, I began exploring the yards of the houses I delivered to. Not the houses themselves. I tried a doorknob and found it locked. Something told me breaking down one of those doors would make me long for the burning. Maybe, I thought, I'd become trapped, forever tormented by the sound of mail hitting a floor, my memories all contained in a book in a house that would now belong to another mailman.

No, never the houses. But the yards seemed harmless enough. Not that I found a lot. But in an entire subdivision of homes, the occasional surprise awaited.

The first was a little red wagon. The most stereotypical child's toy possible kind of red wagon. Shaking my head at my Postmaster's lack of imagination, I pulled the wagon to my bicycle, though a part of me I kept smothered whispered that wagons meant children and children meant delivering feverish and confessional letters to kids.

It took some doing, and the sacrifice of one of my shirts, but I got the wagon tied to the bicycle and spent the day towing my little caboose, now carrying the mail bag, around town. It was fun, though the thought of tortured children, alone with no adult to comfort them, no one to drive out the monster at the mailbox, crept closer and closer, growing larger in my mind until I took the wagon back to its home, carefully leaving it where, and as, I found it.

I found a doghouse at another home. Again, as stereotypical as can be, white roof and red sides, with

"Bowser" written on a board and nailed across the top. Unfortunately, Bowser wasn't home. I checked the doghouse daily and he never appeared to be home. I warmed a Hungry Man Pot Roast dinner and placed it in front of Bowser's house, like a sacrifice. The next day it was still there, cold, congealed, and obviously untouched. Maybe Bowser didn't like pot roast. Couldn't blame him.

I deposited the gloopy TV dinner in the metal trash bin I found next door. The following day it was gone and the bag had no traces of having been stained by gravy. If purgatory had a mailman, maybe it had a trashman too, though this being the only can I ever saw aside from the one inside my own home, which also seemed to refresh daily, it seemed an even more boring job than mine.

Things continued this way for a time (Week? Month? Millennia?) as I came to realize that *everything* in this place was a stereotype, as if whoever, or whatever, made this place had only television shows from the '50s to pull from. This could be *Leave It to Beaver* or *Father Knows Best* (those, for some reason, I remembered vividly). When you looked, really looked, the veneer of reality vanished, like one of those optical illusions where the picture looked like an hourglass until you saw the two faces and then could never make that hourglass appear again. From that point, it was always faces. That was this place. It was three dimensional, so not quite a wooden Hollywood soundstage, but close.

My explorations turned up nothing else interesting. More '50s suburbia porn. Lawn gnomes, plastic flamingoes, at one house an American flag that I patriotically saluted because why the hell not? I might have been a patriot before, or even a soldier. I couldn't remember.

That was, until I explored the yard around 320 Sycamore.

# Four: 320 Sycamore

I thought I'd seen another doghouse but it ended up being a small wellhouse (that particular hourglass remaining an hourglass). I began to walk away, discouraged at not having the chance to lure another Bowser, or Fido or Rover considering the place's penchant for '50s pap, with some tasty pot roast. Then I saw the movement out of the corner of my eye. A twitch of the blinds. Someone looking out to spy on the mailman. The proof of a living soul in this place! Assuming I didn't imagine it. It wasn't something I could ignore even if the chance was small.

The next few days I watched closely as I delivered to 320 Sycamore, even trying to peek into the mail slot once, seeing only a dim '50s suburban household setup. But no sign of life, or of being lived in. My slim letterbox view didn't let me see down to know if the mail was gone. I was discouraged, but not done.

The next day, I didn't just insert the mail into the slot but gave it a push. I looked into the slot to satisfy myself that I'd propelled the mail far enough from the door to see it and, yes, there it lay on the floor about two feet away. I had my bait in place. Let's see if I could lure out a mouse. Or at least confirm the existence of one.

The following morning I bypassed every other house on my route, my bicycle cards whirring furiously as I pedaled toward 320 Sycamore, its mail stuffed into my shirt. The other houses could wait. I was on a mission. Probably not from God, I thought to myself. I knew that was a quote from... something. It wasn't not from any of the books on my shelf. Those I remembered. This was something from before. And before was increasingly becoming never inside my mind. I made a mental note to write it in my notebook. Maybe it would come back to me. Things did sometimes. Not often, but sometimes.

As I approached 320 Sycamore, I watched the windows. No blinds twitched. No watcher today. But the test was a success. The mail was gone from the place where it landed the day before. I looked around my narrow field of view, trying to remember as many details as possible to see if anything else was moved. It took a minute or more of scanning before I registered the tea cup. Sitting on the end table beside the massive recliner, was the kind of tiny, fragile teacup only brought out when company came, practically begging to be held with pinkie extended.

I strained to picture the house in my mind. Was it possible the teacup was there before? Maybe. I was too interested in the possibility of life to worry overmuch about tea, and it fit so perfectly into the 1950s aesthetic of the place that I could have missed it before. But I didn't think so. For some reason that teacup jogged a memory; a stale-smelling drawing room, a kindly old woman, crumbly shortbread cookies. She was my grandmother, I think. Or a favorite aunt. That part I didn't remember. But I was sure she was someone from before. Someone important.

And I was sure, as powerful as that memory was, there was no way I'd have missed that teacup.

I put my mouth to the slot. "Hello! Hello! Mailman here! I saw you yesterday in the window. You took the mail. I know you're in there!" I thought I heard a shuffle and a caught breath.

"Please," I said, much more desperate than was wise. "Please... There isn't anyone else. Not that I've seen. Please. I just want to know you're there. I just want... I just want to know I'm not alone here."

A definite hitched breath that time. A muffled sob, as if a mouth pressed into a towel to stifle sound? Not surprising, I suppose, since I might have been the devil to the person inside this home. I knelt a few more minutes, looking through the letterbox, occasionally calling out. But I saw no movement. I heard no more indication of life.

I went around to the back of the house but I knew what I'd see. These homes were all exactly the same. None had a back door. There were windows here but the blinds were closed tightly. This was behind the soundstage. It didn't require fleshing out.

I couldn't see or hear movement. Whoever was in there had gone silent; whatever emotion I'd evoked, sorrow; regret;

fear; managed now, the house by all appearances as dead as the others.

I finally gave up, shoving the mail through the slot hard enough to again get distance while shouting "here's your mail!" in as cheerful a voice as I could muster. I pedaled back to my house, dejected, picked up my saddlebag and delivered the rest of the mail. I watched as I delivered to 318 and 322 Sycamore but 320 now seemed as dead and empty as all of the others.

When I lay down that night to sleep, full from an unexpected ribeye and huge baking potato left in the refrigerator, I wondered groggily if I could expect punishment for coloring outside my lines. The ribeye made me think not, assuming of course that Postmaster and Grocer were the same entity, but I knew I'd accept it. Finding someone else was too big. It felt like something that *should* happen.

I woke the next morning to nothing at all. The mailbag hung on its hook, full of mail waiting to be sorted. There was no pain, no psychological torture, no food missing from the refrigerator. And no more ribeyes, I noted, giving as stern a glare as I could manage to the Hungry Man Pot Roast, which cared not one bit. It seemed kind of anticlimactic. Like it was a dream. Or a hallucination. I'd had neither since arriving here, but there's a first time for everything.

The thought made me shiver and I picked up my notebook, turning to the last entry. Yes! It was there. I hadn't imagined it. Or, if I had, I'd made writing in the journal part of the hallucination. I had previously thought in a kind of abstract way that the journal might be important. It was mainly a way to pass time, a record of my day and a place for me to list out things I remembered but couldn't place (I noted "mission from God?" at the bottom of this last entry). But I was now beyond thankful for it. It was an oasis of permanence in an increasingly temporary world. A method to offload memories to an external device, to ensure they weren't lost. The journal was a stout tether to Before. I was becoming convinced it deserved to be capitalized. It was a physical thing now. A shrinking commodity.

Every day when I delivered to 320 Sycamore I watched

for movement and got none. Either I truly had imagined it or whoever was inside got wise to being watched and stopped. Or they were terrified. This was the most likely answer. Was having their demon look like a regular person more or less terrible for them? More, I think. At least this sort of behavior is expected of a horned and red winged stereotype. If I saw I was being tormented by a human, I'd wonder. Was he acting with freewill? A trapped soul like myself? Do demons look like us? If only I could get 320 Sycamore to come to the door I could get answers. But he, or she, wasn't answering. They dutifully picked up the mail each day, but despite watching for long minutes, once even leaving and attempting to sneak back and catch a glimpse when they weren't looking, they stubbornly didn't appear.

It was time to escalate.

# Five: Another Day, Another Plan

First I went back and got the red wagon. It was right where I left it so I decided if there was a kid in the house, he didn't come outside to miss it anyhow. After tying it to my bicycle, sacrificing another shirt (there was always another in the closet the next morning), I pedaled over to pick up the metal trash can. Fortunately it wasn't attached to anything so it went into the wagon and I pedaled to 320 Sycamore carrying the tools of my deception.

Parking my bicycle near the door, I stood to the left side of it holding the trash can, my eyes scanning the window for any sign of movement. Satisfied I wasn't being watched, I tossed the trash can down the steps and screamed in what I hoped was my best "man falling down stairs" impression. A few excruciating seconds passed when I got what I wanted, a bend in the blinds and a barely visible hint of dark skin.

Ready for this eventuality, I quickly knelt before the door and peered into the letterbox. I was rewarded with a sight of bare feet sprinting to the back, feminine legs disappearing into a skirt. Then she was gone. But at least I *knew* there was someone, and that someone was a she. I continued to look into the letterbox for signs of movement and got none.

"Hey!," I yelled. "Hey! Come on out. I saw you. I know you're there. Why won't you come out? I think we're all there is. I think whatever this is, we're all that's left. Please..." So close to another life in a dead world I couldn't help being overcome. "I don't want to be alone anymore."

From the back of the house came a voice. "Go away," she said with a tremble. But it didn't sound like fear. More like sadness. And surprisingly calm for it. Resignation? "Go away. Whatever you want from me, I'm not interested." Making effort to hide that tremble. She was brave. I had to give her that.

"I don't want anything," I pleaded. "I just want to talk to you. I just want to hear a voice that isn't mine. To see a human face to prove I'm not alone."

"You're hearing a voice," she said, the voice changing, hard as granite, sharp as coral. "That proves you aren't alone.

That will have to be enough." A pause. I was about to begin my pleading anew when she began again. "Deliver the mail and go. You can't be here. You shouldn't be here. Go away!" The steel began to soften, that tremble in her voice becoming a hitch.

"Don't you miss it," I asked. "Don't you miss interaction? Don't you miss other people?"

"What difference if I did? I'm not coming out there. I'm in Hell, for some reason. I guess I was a bad person once. So give me your damned torture letters and Get. Off. My. Porch." Resignation again. Then back to steel.

It was jarring, the emotional bounce. Like someone fighting with her own mind. "I don't know if this is Hell," I said, giving up on seeing her and sitting beside the door, a finger holding the letterbox open. "I don't know what this is. But I'm not your torturer. Not intentionally. I just deliver the mail. I have to or bad things happen. I don't even know *why* I deliver the mail. Maybe I did once. I don't think so, but..."

"...but you forget things." she broke in. "You're forgetting it all." Not a question.

"Yes," a whisper now. I wondered if she could hear me. "Yes. I'm forgetting. Everything. And I'm afraid."

A shuffling noise. It took all of my will not to dive for the letterbox. But this was more than I'd hoped for by far. From here, I had to be patient or risk losing all. I had to let her make the next move. "You should be afraid," she whispered, right next to the door now.

My finger twitched. I couldn't help it. But before my body could betray me, she spoke, hard again. "No. Stay where you are. If I even think you're about to look in, the conversation ends now. Can you follow rules, mailman?" Her voice was a confusing mix of stern and... fond? Surely not. I couldn't imagine she had any fondness for me, a man she knew nothing about beyond the delivery of terrible letters. But the way she said "mailman" was so familiar.

"Yes," I said, knowing I meant it. A voice was better than nothing. "Yes. I can follow rules. Just... please don't go."

"That would be the smart thing for both of us if I did," she said. "*This place* has rules too. You have to know that by now."

Wincing at the memory of the burning pain, of the single letter on my bed, I nodded, though she couldn't see. "Yes. Yes, I've run afoul of those rules a time or two."

"Good. Then you know why we can't be doing this." I tried to place her accent. There was a lilt that sounded familiar. Kansas? Kentucky? Kenya? Someplace with a K. She paused then. So long that I feared she had left again and was about to call out when I heard a muffled thump, her sitting back to the door, a few inches of wood and insulation separating me from what all evidence pointed to being the only woman in the world.

"All this does is get one of us hurt, Mailman. Or both of us hurt. Whoever, whatever, runs this place has the same regard for us as a kid burning ants with a magnifying glass. I can hear it in your voice. You know how hard this can go."

I was too overcome to do more than whisper. "I don't care."

"Can't hear you, Mailman," she said, that accent getting thicker. "Prop the flap open with the mail. I assume you have some."

I was miserable. "You know I do."

"I do know. So you take my letters and some others and prop that slot open. Do NOT look. I have rules too."

I did as she asked, being very careful that none of the mail dropped inside. She was right about rules and I wasn't keen on finding out what the penalty for delivering letters to the wrong house was. Even accidentally. Not looking was the hardest thing I'd ever done. But I did as she asked and settled back down with my back to hers.

"Now, Mailman. That's better. What were you saying?"

"I said I don't care."

A pause. "Then you're an idiot. Do you know how much torture a body can endure if it doesn't die? You're already a corpse, Mailman. Whoever is holding us here can chop you into bits from your toes up and you'll feel it all. Then you'll wake up whole in your bed like it never happened."

I knew she was right. And I knew I meant it when I said I didn't care. But the specificity of that torture made me curious. "Did something like that happen to you? Did he... it... hurt you too?"

"Lotta ways to hurt, mailman." I heard her sigh. "Some will make you wish you were being skinned alive instead. You need to leave me whichever of those letters is mine and go home. Leave it be, mailman. Leave it while it can still be left."

That tone. "You know something, don't you? You know about this place."

"I don't know anything, mailman," I could hear the lie, but knew better than to call her on it. "And if I did, it would mean less than nothing. You're assuming the rules stay the same here. I think he makes the rules up to suit him."

"Him?" I was amused. "So it's a guy doing all this then?"

"Can't anybody but a man think of something this fucked up."

I felt like I should stick up for my sex, despite remembering almost nothing of what my sex did Before. But that tingle, the one that told me I knew something but couldn't quite grasp it, said she wasn't wrong. "Yeah."

We sat in silence, the brief moment of levity abolished by quiet consent."What could be worse than being alone?" I said. "Than being the only person in the world and forgetting there was ever such a thing as other people? Than becoming the Incredible Clockwork Mailman? If the choice is death, permanent death, I'll take that risk."

She sighed, part exasperation, part resignation. Again. She *did* know something. I gave brief consideration to the possibility this was the Cosmic Postmaster. But no. This was a victim, or one hell of an actor. "You don't get that choice," she said. "What if he doesn't kill us? What if we change? What then? You'll forget me eventually. Or I'll forget you. But how bad will it be until we do?"

This part had never occurred to me. The prospect terrified. "I won't forget you. I've already written you down in my journal."

The pause lingered, though I heard her murmur something I couldn't quite catch. The word "different," I thought. "Come again? I didn't catch that last part."

"You weren't supposed to catch that last part,

Mailman..."

"Could you please stop calling me Mailman?"

I could hear the smile in her voice. "What's your name then... Not Mailman?"

I could have lied. I should have lied. I should have said John or Larry or Ezekiel or even Sue (Sue? A man named Sue? That needed to go in the journal). But I had a feeling she'd know so I told the truth, hesitant. "I don't know my name. I haven't since I got here. I don't think. It's not in my book."

"Then it's kind of hard to call you anything else, Mailman, now isn't it?"

"Do you remember your name? Your past?"

Another pause. I don't know if it was a long one. Every second felt like a year. "My name's Lydia. Beyond that. I don't know much." She sounded as if she was fighting tears. And losing.

"Lydia. I like that. I think I knew a Lydia once. Or maybe she was on TV. I think she was nice." I realized how lame it sounded as soon as I said it.

"Maybe. I don't have a journal like you do." Was that jealousy? Bewilderment? I had forgotten how much body language played in the way things were interpreted. "I have nothing to write with. Besides, the mail disappears the morning after I read it."

I realized I was whispering again, having no more luck at holding back tears than she was. "So when it's gone from your memory..."

"It's gone for good, Guy Who Doesn't Want to be Called Mailman. There's a hole where it used to be, for a while, but then you start to forget the hole too."

I thought for a minute and did the only thing I could. "I could share with you. Pass you the journal to write in and you could pass it back when I deliver the mail next day."

"NO!" The force, the panic, behind it caused me to jump. "No." Calmer now. "Don't you realize the gift you have there? You get to keep some of your memories. I told you what happens to the mail. How could I ever forgive myself if I woke up tomorrow and your book disappeared with the mail? How could you ever forgive me? It would be like..."

"Like killing me."

"No. Killing you would be kinder, mailman. A gunshot to the head is quick."

"Just... not 'Mailman', please. Anything but Mailman."

She paused a moment. "Ok, Donald. I can't take your book. As much as I want it." She did. She sounded hungry.

"Donald?"

"You needed a name. Besides, there's a fragment of memory that says Donald goes well with Lydia. Maybe it's that same TV lady you knew."

"Now that you mention it, I think it was a song... maybe?"

"YES!" It was the first happiness I'd heard in her voice since I found her. "Donald and Lydia!' It was a song! Don't remember who by."

Without even knowing I was doing it, I began to sing. "They made love in the mountains, they made love in the streams, they made love in the valleys...."

"...they made love in their dreams." she finished, losing the battle for composure. She couldn't sing. But that off-key voice was the most beautiful thing I'd ever heard. "That's us, alright," she said once the song had died on our tongues. "Donald and Lydia. I don't know you well enough to be making love to you in my dreams, but that's what this is. Ten miles away. Or at least one door that's just as far in all that matters."

"It doesn't have to be..."

She sniffled. "Yes it does, Mailma-, Donald. I'm going to take this letter on top here," I heard her slide one envelope through, "and let you get on with your route. Go write me down in your book tonight. But don't come asking for me anymore. We weren't meant to meet, Donald."

"Why? How can you know that? Maybe this is how it is supposed to happen. Maybe there isn't any *supposed to* involved."

"No. I know. You need to trust me on this. We aren't supposed to meet. I *know*. Goodbye, Postman Donald." With that, the other mail slid out onto the porch and the flap closed. I sat staring at them for a moment then opened the letterbox to look through. As I knew would be the case, she'd already left.

From the back of the house I heard "But I'm glad we did."

I delivered the mail. What else could I do? I suppose I should have been curious about the other houses, on the lookout for other signs of life. But I went through the motions of shoving envelopes into slots until I was done, then pedaled home to write in my journal.

## Six: Curiouser

I'd like to think I could never forget Lydia. She was certainly all I thought about now. Not romantically. Not then. But I knew better. So I wrote in a fever, covering several of those never-ending pages with all I could remember of her, from her accent to her phrases to her calling me Donald to singing the song together. By the end I was spilling tears on the pages, smudging the pencil lead. If I had any bravery at all, I'd give her the book despite her refusal. But she was right. The book had all of me in it. The book WAS me. I couldn't risk it.

I put the book down, picked moreosely at my Hungry Man Pot Roast, and went to bed.

I woke an instant later, as I always did. By all indication, it was a day like any other one. Morning sunlight through the window, the mailbag hanging on its hook. I fumbled for my book and turned to the last entry. There it all was. Every detail about the day before. Lydia was real. We'd interacted. We'd made a connection over a song.

And she never wanted to see me again.

So, for the third time since I awoke in this place, an Operation took shape. Operation Gift.

Knowing a bit about Lydia now made me feel even more guilty about delivering those letters to her. She hadn't said what was in them but she hadn't really made a secret of them not being pleasant. So I decided I would bring her packages, nicer ones, until she spoke again, or at least until I stopped feeling guilty. Or ran out of gifts skinny enough to fit in a letterbox.

I looked around the house. The most valuable things I owned beside my journal were the books on my shelf. They'd all been read, some multiple times. They were a rare link to Before. But it was something. I thought for a moment that leading with my best gift might be a bad thing, but I also didn't think I had time for traditional courting. I grabbed *Alice in Wonderland*, my favorite of the books, and stuffed it into my mailbag.

I went on my route as normal, resisting the urge to head straight for 320 Sycamore. It was as close to a highlight as my day had. I needed to savor the anticipation.

When I got to Lydia's house, I had to fight not to throw myself at the door, to call her name over and over until she answered me or my voice gave out. She'd made it clear she didn't want to hear from me again and I sensed she wasn't one who reacted well to being pushed. If I wanted that to change, if there was even a chance it could, I had to let her come to me.

I walked up to the door as normally as I could, but I was shaking. When I got there I looked at the windows but saw no indication she was watching. I resisted the urge to look through the letterbox. I just dropped off the mail and, after a moment of selfish doubt, pushed *Alice in Wonderland* through as well.

I paused briefly, thinking the louder noise would draw her. It didn't that I could tell, so I went about my route and went home to write in my journal.

The next day I picked out *Brief History of Time*, sure it wouldn't fit but hoping maybe if I opened it I could shove it through. I tossed *Fall of the House of Usher* into the bag just in case.

When I approached 320 Sycamore I immediately noticed something on the porch. Excited, I hurried up the stairs and scooped it up. I stared down at a copy of *Jane Eyre* and smiled. Not so disinterested as she let on then. I pulled *Brief History of Time* out of my bag and, with some effort to get the pages even and a little muscle, I pushed it through the slot, hearing a weighty thump as it hit the carpet. Again, I heard no indication she was near. But *Jane Eyre* said all I needed to know.

So began the Afterlife Inter-Library Loan Society. I didn't bring a book every day, knowing they were limited and I should draw them out, but once a week or so I'd bring another to push through the slot and sometimes I'd find another on the porch. *Brief History of Time* for *Little Women*. *Journey to the Centre of the Earth* for *A Wrinkle in Time*. *The Maltese Falcon* for *The Big Sleep*.

It provided something to do, but didn't get me any more interaction from Lydia. I wasn't even sure if she read the books, though I knew how I devoured them, craving even the most fantastic stories of Before. That was, until I'd delivered four books, a month as time reckoned here, which meant not at all.

I walked up to 320 Sycamore and saw a slim volume on the step. I hadn't brought a book that day, but our gifting didn't always match up so that wasn't a problem. When I picked up the book, excited at where the pages would take me next, I was surprised to look down and see... *Alice in Wonderland*.

As I opened the mail slot to insert the letters I heard from next to the door "That was a good one, mailman."

I froze, the mail falling from my hand into the house. "So you're talking to me again?"

"I guess. I oughtn't be. That hasn't changed. But the book was good. I *felt* it so much. I needed to talk about it."

I sat down, my back to the door, propping the letterbox open with the book. I remembered the rules when I had to. "You felt *Alice in Wonderland*? I can't remember Before very clearly, but I'm fairly confident white rabbits with pocket watches played no part in it."

"Exactly." If I'd hoped my joke would get a laugh, I failed. Instead she sounded sad, as she often did. "Out of all the books on your shelf, does any explain this place better than Alice's rabbit hole?"

"No," I admitted. "I'm glad you liked the book. I liked it too. It's my favorite one."

We sat like that for no time, and all time, discussing poor silly Alice and her poor silly adventures.

I told her about my theory that the whole book was one faulty logic puzzle, an intentional misinterpretation of data to come to a wrong conclusion. She laughed, finally, her voice becoming animated, and told me that nothing ruined a nice children's story like math. Then it got serious.

"Sometimes I feel like Giant Alice," she said. "I think I'll cry until I create a giant river of tears for everyone to swim in."

"Yeah. I haven't seen any 'Eat Me' cakes that helps me find the door out of here yet."

"No." We let the silence linger.

"Look, I know you don't think we should talk, but..."

"Not happening, Donald. We've been over this."

"Hear me out," I said, a little more exasperated than was warranted. "We've both got new books. What could it hurt to talk about the books?"

Pause. "Nothing else... I swear, you try to trick me, mailman, and you'll never hear from me again AND I'll keep all your books."

While it wasn't what I wanted, it was what I could get. "Yes. Just the books. I read *Jane Eyre* this week. Maybe we could discuss it tomorrow?" The question sounded like a plea.

"Why don't you bring it back tomorrow so I can brush up. Then we can both talk about it fresh. This time next week?"

I smiled. "It's a date!"

A sharp intake of breath, and a pause. "No, Donald. It's not a date. Please don't."

"It's just a turn of phrase. I didn't mean--"

"You did. And you know you did. Don't lie to me."

"It's a chat about books with a friend?"

"Better. I guess we are friends now." I could hear the smile. "It's the strangest book club I've ever been in."

"Have you ever even been in a book club?"

"I don't know if I was ever in a book club Before. But I'd put money on this being the weirdest one if I had."

"Yeah."

And that's how the Afterlife Inter-library Loan Society became the Afterlife Bi-Weekly Book Club.

# Seven: The Afterlife Bi-Weekly Book Club

Do afterlife apocalyptic alien worlds have highlights? Does Hell (I was starting to believe this might be, even with the coffee) have moments of joy? If so, those were it. I vaguely remembered sneering at book clubs in the Before, finding dull discussion groups about books you were required to read to take any pleasure I might have had out of reading. But when your only interaction with another person was that bi-weekly book club, you came to love it. As I suspected I was coming to love Lydia.

Yes, I know. Only woman in the world. Pretty easy to crush on when there isn't anyone else. It was as stereotypical a trope as this place was. But it wasn't that. If I had a "type" I think she'd be it. Funny, sarcastic, acerbic when it was needed, tender at surprising times. Her personality fascinated me and our book club sessions were long and spirited and I wondered if she was developing feelings for me or if the book club was truly just a chance to talk to her Mailman.

I knew what I had to do next, but didn't act on it. Not at first. We were three months, or whatever counts as months here, into Book Club, six books for sure, before I made my move. The time only confirmed what I felt. Deepening it. I only hoped my patience would be rewarded and the odd and one-sided courtship ritual wasn't futility.

At the end of one particularly animated book club discussion, about the differences and similarities between Hammett's Sam Spade and Chandler's Phillip Marlowe, I decided to go for it. "I want to see you," I blurted out, abandoning my well-planned smooth lead in. "I *need* to see what you look like."

She didn't answer for a time. "Not a good idea, Donald. You and I both know if I open this door either I'm coming out or you're coming in and that's going to ruin it all. Just imagine the most beautiful woman in the world and that's me. It might be true here."

"It's not fair. You know what I look like. Why can't I see you? You don't have to open the door. Just pull the blinds up and I can see you through the window."

"No go, Mailman." She reverted to that when she was annoyed. "Blinds don't go up. There's a cord, but it doesn't do anything."

I thought for a minute. "I could look through the letterbox."

A small laugh. "Boy, those are some sexy hipbones you have there, lady. I can't see anything else through this little hole but man are those hips *fire.*"

I felt a hint of annoyance. Normally I enjoyed her sarcastic wit. But today I was so close to what I wanted, or as close to what I wanted as could get, that I wasn't in the mood for jokes. "Stand back some, like beside that couch. I think I could see all of you from that far."

"This is a serious mistake, Donald." She sounded conflicted, which I took as a good sign. Anything not a no could be made a yes with enough patience. "You know the rules. I don't know what He will do to us if you look."

"He did nothing when you looked at me, did he?" She hadn't specifically said He didn't, but I took the gamble.

"No. He didn't." A sigh and shuffling feet. "Have your peep show, Mailman. But only for a few seconds."

"That's fine. Let me know when you're ready."

The drawl she used when she was being particularly acerbic. "I ain't taking my clothes off. This isn't that kind of peep show."

"I'm too much of a gentleman to even consider it." I put on my most proper English voice.

A giggle from across the room. "I don't know if I'd go that far. But I'm here. Have your look."

I bent to the letterbox and looked in. She had moved far enough away for me to see all of her. And had turned on the desk lamp, my first indication she had electricity too.

The breath left me. Mocha skin, black hair that fell to her shoulders. Not skinny, exactly, but not fat. My brain conjured 'voluptuous' as an appropriate word. Her body was well-covered by a simple cotton dress, but accentuated more for its obscuring. I didn't remember any women from the Before, but I knew this one was beautiful. Not that it mattered.

She could have looked like Frankenstein (where did that come from? I wrote it down later that night, but it never came back) and she'd have looked perfect to me. I knew then, if I didn't before, that I had fallen hopelessly for this woman, and that she was almost certainly giving me the closest chance I'd have to act on it.

I wolf whistled. "Daaaamn, girl. You're looking good."

"You haven't seen a women for eternity, Mailman," she said and I finally got to see that smile light up her face. "You go long enough without and anything with a convenient orifice will do. I remember that much about men."

"No, it's not that," I stammered and knew I meant it. I'd never gotten an erection since coming here that I could remember. I didn't even know if those parts worked. "This isn't me thinking with my little head. You really are beautiful."

"Thanks, Mailman... Donald. Now show and tell is over. Get to delivering that mail." She moved to the side, out of my narrow view.

"But... we've got to talk about this, don't we? We can't let it hang."

"Nothing to talk about." She was in her usual spot beside the letterbox now. "You've got a face to put to the voice. Let it be enough." This last sounded sad, like she wanted it to happen no more than I. "Rules."

I gave up. "Goodbye, Lydia. You know how to get me if you want to talk more. Otherwise..."

"You'll see me in two weeks. *House of Usher* next go?"

"Yeah. *The Fall...*" I turned and began to walk away.

I heard the mail flap open. "I'm glad you saw me. I'm glad we had that, little as it is."

"Me too," I whispered, pulling 319 Sycamore's mail from the bag and willing myself not to look back.

Back in my house I wrote as detailed a description of her as I could in my journal. I even tried, briefly, to sketch her. I don't know if I could draw Before, but I sure couldn't now. I didn't know if I'd ever see her again and I didn't want to forget it. Not ever.

# Eight: The Final Gift

That night, my Cosmic Grocer brought me a dozen eggs. I resisted eating them all at once, taking the gamble they wouldn't disappear. For almost a week I had eggs every day. Fried eggs. Scrambled Eggs. Hard-boiled. Soft-boiled. Omelets. I went into mourning when I cracked the last two. The next day I threw the Hungry Man Pot Roast across the room, still frozen. It thunked against the wall and sat there silently, like it knew I'd have to come crawling back. Worst part? I knew it was right.

I wished I could share the eggs with Lydia. I briefly considered dropping an omelet through the slot but wasn't sure I could get it through without falling off the plate and it seemed worse to imply Lydia should eat my leftovers from the floor than to just not give them at all.

Then I remembered Operation Gift. Success in starting the library and later the book club made me forget about my original plan to bring her things other than the mail, to drop off more pleasant things than those damned letters. Problem was, I was working with limited space. There were only so many things that would go inside a mail slot. That's why I started with the book. I looked around for something I could bring her; something flat enough to fit through a mail slot. There wasn't a lot in my house. My playing cards would work, but I had no idea if she had some and, if she did, I would have wasted my limited entertainment and gained her nothing.

Then my eyes fell on the Hungry Man Pot Roast Dinner (With Apple Crumble Dessert!). It lay there on the floor taunting me, reminding me that it *might* fit through a mail slot. And, unlike my cards, I had plenty to spare.

I couldn't believe I was even thinking it. As if those taunting letters weren't enough, I would prove myself the demon by bringing one of those?

This started one of my famous "one-man debates." You try living alone for eternity. You've got to have *someone* to argue with. Maybe she had some other food. Maybe she had all the Hungry Man Salisbury Steaks I used to have. I remembered how refreshing the Pot Roast was for a day or two, just by being anything that wasn't Salisbury Steak.

Besides, the devil on my shoulder said, what did I have to lose? One Hungry Man Pot Roast of a limitless supply. Possibly the respect of the woman I was coming to love, but that was a risk I had to take.

The next morning I wrapped one of the Hungry Man Pot Roast Dinners in a towel with a zip top bag full of ice and tucked it in with my mail. Not wanting my frozen gift to be a soggy thawed one, I rode straight to 320 Sycamore and, carrying her letters in one hand and my frozen dinner in the other, I walked up to the door and dropped first the letters and then the dinner. It fit, just. I heard it thunk on the floor and bang against the door, briefly hoping she was awake to get it before it thawed.

Then, from just the other side of the door, from her usual book club spot, I heard a barked laugh. "Lydia?" I asked.

"Did you just gift me a TV dinner, mailman?" She giggled.

I smiled. "Yeah, I guess I did. Happy birthday?"

"How do you know it's my birthday?"

"Do you know when your birthday is?"

A pause. Then resignation. "You know I don't."

"Then Happy Birthday."

"You sure know how to show a girl a good time, Donald. You must have been quite the lady killer Before."

Now I was chuckling too. "I don't remember dating Before. But I'm pretty sure I had more space to work with. This slot limits my material."

She had given up giggling and was laughing outright now. "You could have at least brought candles!"

"I have matches. You could stand them up in the apple crumble!" I was losing control now; laughing so hard it was difficult to catch my breath.

"Extra sulfur smell.... for that... special someone's birthday... IN HELL!" The fit had completely taken her over.

"Bet your mailman Before never delivered you food!" I fell next to the door. My ribs hurt.

"You could have...." More laughter. "You could have at

least brought me a PIZZA!"

I couldn't answer for near thirty seconds for laughing. "I've been all over this subdivision, darling. There's nary a Domino's to be found."

The conversation stopped then. We were both laughing too hard. An occasional gasped quip like "hold the anchovies!" would slip out before the giggle fits took us again.

As I regained a bit of my composure I made my move. "I love you."

She cut off mid-laugh. "Don't say that to me. Don't ever say that to me again. Please?" Pleading. Common from my side of the door. New from hers.

"I do. At least I think I do. You're all I think about. When I'm delivering mail, when I'm sitting in my house. My journal is full of you. *I'm* full of you."

I was alarmed to hear the laughter turn to sobs. No words, just sobs. She wasn't even trying to hide them anymore, any attempts at being brave lost.

"I'm sorry. I know you probably don't feel that way. I... I understand. Can we still be friends?"

I could hear her choke back the sobs and when she spoke her voice was as angry as I'd heard. "You are the biggest dumbass in all of the afterlife Donald T. Postman!"

A confused look crossed my face. "I probably am. But... what's that got to do with me I---"

"No! Don't say it again. Else I go."

"I'm sorry."

The voice softened. "You think I'm not feeling this too? You think I'm just sitting over here for months talking and laughing and spending time with a guy who's funny and sweet and kind of cute in that uniform and feeling *nothing?*" You must think I'm the one who's the devil."

"Never."

"Good. Because I do love you, if love comes into any of this. Or I think I'm starting to. I don't want to. I shouldn't. We've got letterbox love, Mailman. We can only have whatever fits in this slot." She paused then and put on a false flippancy. "I guess you could stick your willie in the slot and I'll see what I can do."

"Please. Don't do that. You know this isn't about sex. I don't even know if sex works here."

She sounded sad again. "I don't either." The tone different there. Maybe she was just prudish. Maybe she did know. "I wish I could find out with you, Donald. I do. But this is what we have. I open this door... it's over. Maybe... *maybe*, we get one night, and then what?"

"Maybe we get all the nights?" I whispered.

"No. We don't."

The absolute conviction in her voice stopped me. "You can't know that."

"I can." She sighed. "I do. You do too. In your bones. It's another thing you've forgotten. I don't want to lose what we've got right now. I don't want to lose the book club or waiting for you to walk up the drive or any of it. I want the speculative. But I can't lose the guaranteed. Can I?" The weight of it hung like fog.

"So what do we do now?" My own voice fog-hazed.

The pause seemed to go on forever. "Now we sleep on it. We've got decisions to make, Donald. And none of them good. Deliver your mail. Go home. Sleep. Let's talk tomorrow."

"But..."

"No." She sounded sad, but firm. "We can't do something like this without considering it. Without considering what we might give up. What we *will* give up." That odd certainty again. "Go home. Write it in your journal. Think about me."

"I always think about you."

"That makes it worse." Can tears be heard? I thought I did.

"Try it from my side sometime."

The conversation stalled. "Ok. I'm going to... go deliver the mail now. I'll see you tomorrow."

"Where we'll figure the rest of it out."

I began to walk slowly away from the door, wanting so badly to go back and batter the door down.

Through the mail slot I heard "Donald?"

I turned, hopeful.

"Thanks for the food."

"I hope you enjoy it. I stopped enjoying the damned things about 200 meals ago." I turned again.

"WAIT!" she screamed. I walked back to the door, hearing her run. The feet padded back and a package fell out on my toes.

"Stouffer's Lasagna? Is this..."

"All I ever eat. That pot roast is going to taste like filet tonight."

Could frozen lasagna be more than noodles and sauce? It could. It *was*. "Same."

We stalled there.

"Well, thanks. I'll enjoy it."

"I hope so. Enjoy it and think of me."

"I always..."

She interrupted. "You already said that Mailman. Go deliver the mail before you bore me to tears saying the same stuff over and over." A sliver of light in the darkness of her voice.

I walked away a second time and this time she didn't call me back. I rode back to the house and carefully set the Stouffer's Lasagna in the freezer on top of the Hungry Man stack.

Then I delivered the mail. Some things didn't change. I wanted nothing in this world but her. That included those damned letters.

She said to sleep on it, but I didn't want to. Tomorrow was unknown, and terrifying for it. Every day in this place was one giant routine. I got up, I read, I delivered the mail. Maybe I went for a run. Tonight I ate the lasagna. She was right. It tasted like gourmet cuisine. Tomato sauce was amazing! I basked in the simplicity of difference. I wrote in my journal.

I wrote about Book Club.

I felt a certainty it was all over. She was right about that. There would be no more Afterlife Bi-Weekly Book Club. We were beyond. Whether she opened the door tomorrow or not, everything changed. We'd meet, finally, or she'd send me away. She said she didn't want what we had to change. But it had changed. I saw no reason not to take the leap.

Win or lose. Here, status quo was the draw. I got the

feeling my Cosmic Jailers had lost their appetites for status quo. Here there was no draw.

I paged through my journal, marking my time since I got it like tree rings. I was bothered by how much I'd forgotten before reading it jogged my memory. Not just Before any longer but Here. So much of it in so little time. Did I really think there might have been a dog? Did I really worry a kid would come for the red wagon? I remembered none of it. But it was in the journal. It happened. It *happened* and I could read about it and remember. Or at least confirm it was real. Confirm I was real.

Whatever happened tomorrow, I'd have Lydia in my journal. Hopefully to read with her, to laugh together at our naive concepts of how this place worked, sharing a Stouffer's Lasagna one night, a Hungry Man Pot Roast the next. If not, to remember that there is something good in this place, that it's not all just mail and emptiness.

I didn't know that forgetting might not be better in that situation, but I didn't want to. Not her. Forgetting her was, I sensed, the last step to forgetting myself. To eventually forgetting even the journal. To filing it away on the shelf alongside *Jane Eyre,* never knowing that book hadn't always been there. Never knowing that next to *Journey to the Centre of the Earth* was all of me. The Incredible Clockwork Mailman would officially come to life, or mechanical half-life.

Closing my journal I set it where I'd have to see it as soon as I woke. It was the most precious thing I had.

For tonight.

# Nine: A Lady and a Tiger

The next morning I tried to keep my routine. I found an unexpected surprise upon entering my kitchen. A birthday cake. And a box of candles. Looks like someone up there is rooting for the home team. Thanks for the support, Cosmic Grocer. He *was* a different entity than the Cosmic Postmaster. I was convinced of that now. And He was on *my side!*

I wasn't entirely sure how I was getting it to 320 Sycamore, but then I didn't even know if it would be needed for a celebration or for a farewell, a sliver-thin slice shoved through a mail slot.

But first things first. I delivered the mail. If this day ended as I hoped, I was going to be too busy. If it didn't, too depressed. Either way, I didn't want to risk whatever wrath my Postmaster might dole out. Evidence thus far was, however benevolent the Cosmic Grocer was, he either condoned, or couldn't stop, the punishments of the Cosmic Postmaster. "When the rockets go up, who cares where they come down? That's not my department," I sang, not knowing where it came from, or why music was what seemed to come back when it was needed.

Once I finished the mail I pedaled slowly to 320 Sycamore, leaving the cake behind for now, as nervous as a virgin. Which, I guess, I was in this place.

As soon as I walked up and dropped the mail in I heard her voice, from her usual spot beside the door, "What are we going to do about all of this, Mailman?"

"Stop calling me Mailman for a start?"

The mirth in her voice was forced. "What are we going to do about all of this, Mailman Donald?"

"You already know what I want."

She sighed. "We want the same thing. And we *don't* want the same thing. Question we have before us is which do we want, or not want, more?"

I sat across from her, then realized I had no mail and no book. "You're going to have to provide the slot-propper today, I'm afraid."

"Going Dutch on this one, eh? Classy." I heard her get up and move away, then a slim volume prop the flap open. The spine was to me and I could read enough to know what it was.

"Curiouser and curiouser...."

"I thought *Alice in Wonderland* fit. We could be going down the rabbit hole."

I leaned my head against the house, trying to feel her just a few inches away. "Maybe I want to go down the rabbit hole. Alice came out ok."

"You don't know that. The book ended too soon. Alice might have gone crazy. It's what I'd do if I saw rabbits in suits."

I smiled. "Not if you were out here. If I saw a rabbit running by with a pocket watch, I'd probably just think it must be Thursday."

"But what about the rabbit? You're outside the rabbit hole. I'm inside. Alice might be ok, but how would it change the rabbit to live in Alice's world?"

"I think this place's overlord wants us to be together. At least *one* of them does."

"What kind of crazy conspiracy shit have you been writing in that journal of yours, mailman? There are two of them now?"

"I think so. I'm pretty sure that someone, something, out there is rooting for us." I told her about the birthday cake and the candles. "What else could that be? I've been dealing with the Cosmic Postmaster and the Cosmic Grocer for a while now. Neither has really been the joking type. So why taunt us with the birthday cake we just talked about? It's got to be a sign."

"If there are two of them, how do you know the one who wants this has the power?" she said softly.

Silence followed. We could only drag this out so long. Finally, she broke it before it got too heavy. "Did you ever hear that story about the Lady and the Tiger?"

"Did we do that in book club?"

"No. That was from Before."

"I might have read it once..."

"...but you forgot. I can't find a pattern to what you

remember and forget here. I don't even know my own damned *name*, I made Lydia up, but I know this little story. And you don't think whoever runs this has a cruel sense of humor?"

"I was just thinking that on the way up here. I always remember music."

"You always do," she said, sounding by the end like someone who should have shut up a sentence ago.

"What? I always do? Always when?"

"Before the book club. When we sang "Donald and Lydia" together. Did you forget that too?" She'd recovered well, but the lie hung unchallenged all the same.

To cut the tension, I spoke. "Tell me about the Lady and the Tiger."

"Well," she said, "There was this king, or emperor, or something like that. He ruled a land and he had this law where if you got caught doing a crime you were put into a pit with two doors. Behind one was a woman. Behind the other was a tiger. Then you had to choose. If you picked the woman, you married her. If you picked the tiger... Well, it'd do what tigers do."

"So you had to pick between a tiger and a woman you never met before?"

"Yep."

"And you just married her if you opened her door?"

"That's about the size of it."

I chuckled. "So a tiger and another tiger."

"That kind of sexist talk will get you nowhere near what's underneath this tiger's dress, Mailman."

I froze mid-laugh. I didn't want to say the next part, but the time had come. "So you've decided, then." Not a question.

"Not until I take one more chance to remind you that this won't end well."

I felt relief. And fear. And anticipation. And dread. "I'll take the lady and deal with the tiger when I meet her."

# Ten: Doors Open

We were here, finally, and neither of us wanted to be the first to make a move. After a time I heard her shuffling. "Stand up. While the sound of a man in uniform at my feet is appealing, I think we should meet the first time face to face. Don't you?"

I stood and faced the door. "You sure you want to do this?"

"No," came the reply. "But I'm going to anyway. Get the book. We don't need it anymore."

I slid the book out of the mail slot and into my pocket. The knob turned and the door opened, like a curtain pulled back on the last act of a play.

The memory of seeing her before hadn't faded, in part because I read my description of it in the journal every night. But it didn't prepare me for a 3D unletterboxed Lydia. I wasn't sure what to say next. She stepped onto the porch and seemed to be having the same problem, as we came to terms with this new reality. I'd waited for this moment for what felt like eternity (and, I supposed, it might have been) and I suspected she had for a lot longer than she let on. The hesitancy of what to do next ended as she fell into me.

A couple of the more melodramatic books in my collection talked about "a kiss for the ages" or "a kiss that shook the Earth" but this was a different place than Before, and those hack writers didn't have what I had to work with.

It was the kiss at the end of the world. At the birth of another.

I couldn't tell you how long it lasted. We've established that time is funny here at the best of times and, in this case, I was too distracted to even make an attempt at keeping up. I can tell you it went on forever. It ended too soon.

When we finally broke, we were both a bit too stunned to say anything. When I cleared the mind fog, I decided to break the tension with humor. "Boy, those are some sexy hipbones you have there, lady!"

A look of confusion crossed her face, then she slugged

me. "Ha ha. I didn't order a joke-a-gram."

I leaned in, a hair from her ear. "What did you order, then?"

She leaned away from me and gave me a flat stare. "A willie without a letter slot," she deadpanned.

None of those melodramatic novelists ever had characters' big romantic scenes interrupted by giggle fits. More's the pity them. As much as I hoped the night held the kinds of things those writers *did* get on with, if I could have frozen time there I would have, her weight on my chest as she laughed close to me, my head on her neck as I did the same. You forget how much hearing someone else laugh gets inside you, how it trips just about every pleasure center a brain ever thought of.

"Should I come in?" I asked.

"No!" A strange hint of panic there. "No... I've been stuck in that house for... well for as long as whatever this is has been going on. I want to stretch my legs and see the sights."

"But I've never been inside one of these houses... and I'm sure you've got a bed in there somewhere."

She glowered. "I do, and you won't be climbing in it. I've got the worst case of cabin fever ever and I don't know how much time we have. I want to spend it outside."

I stepped off the porch and bowed. "Welcome to my neighborhood, little Alice."

She walked past me into the street. "I might go all the way on the first date," she shot back. "Especially when I suspect the first date and the last might be the same date." She looked over her shoulder and smiled. "But I *do* expect there to be a date, Mailman. It's the polite thing to do. Besides, it's my birthday. I want a party!" She linked her arm with mine. "Show me the town, Donald."

"Um. This is pretty much it. All of the houses look alike. There's a small green space that I guess might be a park. There's my house. You're welcome over."

"Donald, I have *got* to teach you dating etiquette. You don't lead with 'your place or mine'. Wine and dine a lady first! Show her a good time before you start asking for her to show you one."

I stammered something about not meaning that way. She laughed and pressed a finger to my lips. "You're cute when you're being an idiot. Let's just be together, eh? I know being outside is routine for you, but it's the first time in my... afterlife?" A brief look of pain crossed her face, a tell to an emotion I myself felt all too often. A vague sense of loss for a Before we barely remember.

"Wait!" I shouted. "I've got it! Stay here!" I ran to my bicycle.

"You ditching me already, Mailman?" Another half-smile.

I was already pedaling furiously away. "Just wait there. It will be worth it!"

When I came back, she had wandered a couple houses down, looking at all of the uniform little boxes with a creased forehead. My bicycle cards caused her to look over and break into that wide grin I could fall into for whatever eternity this was.

"Is this your idea of a limo ride?" she said with mock scorn, looking at the red wagon tied to the back of my bicycle with yet another sacrificed shirt.

"Your chariot awaits, my dear."

She shook her head. "There is no way I'm getting inside that thing. I'll crack my skull!"

"And do what? As you've pointed out to me many times, we're already dead."

She grumbled even as she walked over and began to climb into the small wagon. "Not a lot of leg room, I have to say. And not exactly horse-drawn carriage romantic." She paused for effect and just as I was about to break the silence, put on the worst fake demure look ever. "But how many women can say they've been driven around The Great Empty by a shirtless chauffeur? You are even cuter without the uniform, mailman. Something to look forward to, I guess. For now, though, drive on Jeeves, the great city awaits my arrival!"

"Jeeves?"

That look of something just out of reach again. "I think it's from Before. It sounds... right."

I searched my own increasingly hole-ridden memory. "Yeah, it does. C'mon Cleopatra, your subjects await."

And that is how the Afterlife Library Loan Society turned Afterlife Bi-Weekly Book Club became the first Afterlife Blind Date.

I don't ever remember dating Before, so had nothing to compare, but I can't imagine anything better. I dutifully pedaled her around the streets of my all too familiar subdivision, her frequent exclamations at things like the lonely trash can and the dog house reminding me of my own early days here. I'd forgotten that feeling. Another moment lost to everything but the journal.

I pedaled her down hills, picking up speed until the wagon protested and wobbled dangerously. She screamed and laughed like she was on a thrill ride. Then she insisted on switching places.

"Do you even know how to ride a bicycle?" I asked.

"Guess you're about to find out as soon as I do. In the wagon, Mailman."

I got in. "This is a very bad idea."

"Not the first one today. Probably not the last. Let's make it fun." With that she began to pedal, slowly at first, like someone trying to remember how to ride a bike, then faster and I got my own thrill ride. I am not ashamed to admit I was no more brave than her, screaming and laughing at the speed, the instability, of the wagon.

"You scream like a girl," she said as she stopped the bike near the patch of green I'd come to call the park.

"So do you," I said.

"I *am* a girl, Donald. Perhaps you forgot." She smoothed her dress and walked past swaying her hips, and I felt something I had thought dead rising to the occasion.

"That's no girl. That is one hell of a stacked woman."

She gave me her best seductive gaze and slowly worked her way up to me, her hips moving to a music only she heard, but I could imagine.

Then she kissed me again. Not the little pecks she'd doled out after that first kiss but another long, deep, and utterly entrancing one. "You better not forget it. What else you got in this town?"

"Nothing much, I'm afraid. Well, I have birthday cake for you. And, if you want dinner I could warm a couple of Hungry Man Pot Roasts."

She made a face. "Nothing is going to ruin this night like TV dinners and no TV. Just get the cake."

"Back in the wagon!" I yelled. "And on to Casa De Donald!"

She hesitated then. "Ok. But I'm not going inside."
"Why?"

Exasperated, as if talking to a small child. "I already told you. I spent eternity inside and I don't want to see walls again. Besides," she paused here. "we still don't know the rules of this," a vague wave. "Let's not tempt fate. Or your Cosmic Postmaster. Or whoever."

"Ok," I agreed. You can talk to me through the front door while I get your cake ready?"

"That should be safe."

We rode to my house, her in the wagon, me pedaling slowly, letting her take it all in. When we stopped at my house she got out of the wagon and looked at it for a moment. "Yours is different. It doesn't look the same as all the others."

Strange. Despite seeing every house in this neighborhood and this one daily, it's not something I ever took note of before. Or it wasn't that way before. "I guess it is. There are perks to being a civil servant."

"Obviously. Go get my cake. It's my birthday."

I smiled. "Absolutely, birthday girl. You wait right here."

"I ain't going anywhere."

I ran into the house and began putting candles into the cake. As I got my matches, I caught a glimpse of something different. I walked over and saw an old fashioned woven picnic basket. Opening the lid I found all of the fixings for a stereotypical picnic. Sandwiches, potato salad, mac and cheese, even a thermos of coffee. I gave a nod to the Cosmic Grocer. "Still got my back, brother. I forgive you every pot roast dinner you ever sent."

# Eleven: A Birthday to Remember

I walked toward the door and yelled "No cake yet. I have a surprise."

"I want that cake, Mailman. What's this mess?"

I came through the door and handed her the picnic basket, holding up the folded red-check tablecloth that was beneath it. "Courtesy of the Cosmic Grocer."

Tears welled in her and I frowned. This wasn't what I expected. "What? You don't want a picnic? I... I can take it back inside."

She shook her head. "No. No." She sniffled. "I want this. I can't imagine anyone I want this with more. But you're right. Maybe this one will be different." Brief panic, tamped down and covered by a smile.

I wasn't ready to let it go this time. This was important. "*What* one will be different?"

She put her arms straight out and spun. "All of it. Everything that's happened since I got here. This is the first sign of benevolence I've seen. Maybe this isn't Hell after all."

I considered staying on topic, but time was short, or might be. So I dug into the basket and brought out the thermos. "Coffee! I said when I got here that Hell wouldn't have coffee."

"You sure? It's hot... I hope you've got fixings in there. I like my coffee pale and sweet as sin." She looked me over and gave a wicked grin. "Kind of the way I like my mailmen."

Playing along. "I like mine just like I like my women," taking in her ebony skin.

"Ugh," she exclaimed. "Even forgetting Before, I know that joke's moldy. Hot and black, eh?"

"Dark and bitter," I said, barely keeping my voice flat.

She hit me again. "You are an asshole, Mailman." She tucked one arm through the basket handle and the other in mine. "I like you. Let's go have a picnic in the park."

"The cake..."

"We can come back for it. You can't give a birthday girl a cake before she's had lunch. It's not proper protocol."

We went to the greenway and laid out the spread. Over sandwiches (egg salad), bowls of sides, and hot coffee (the sugar and cream were indeed tucked into the bottom of the basket). We talked, of what we remembered from Before. Of Alice in Wonderland, Raymond Chandler, Jules Verne, and even the trashy melodramatic romances, both agreeing it must be a joke on the part of our Cosmic Postmaster or Cosmic Grocer, or perhaps a neutral Cosmic Librarian, their stinkiness in direct contrast with the classics on both our shelves. She lay with her head in my lap, the voice inside my head whispering this itself bordered on so stereotypical it made even those 'barely there boulder holder' (her words, referencing the heaving and unnaturally huge breasts being precariously contained by a distressed blouse on the covers) books seem literary.

After that we just sat for a time; me stroking her face, her laying with a look of total happiness on hers. "Can't we just spend our entire afterlife like this?" I asked. "Maybe we can. It never gets fully dark until..." I frowned, looking at the approaching dusk. "until I finish delivering the mail."

She opened her eyes, taking in the setting sun. "We always knew we were only guaranteed this one day, Donald. Let's not get sad about it. It's the best birthday I ever had. I want to remember that. Now, go get me that cake."

I didn't want to move. "You promise you'll be here when I get back?"

A frown. "You know I can't. But I'm not moving on my own."

Panic as I had a thought. "Sit up! You can't fall asleep."

She stayed laying on the grass. "Wouldn't dream of it Mailman." Another small grin. "Unless you stand there nattering. Go get my cake."

I went back to the house and put the cake carefully in the wagon. When I returned, I only truly began to breathe again as I saw she was still lying there, the bliss still painting her face with beauty. As I approached, she spoke. "Welcome back, Donald. I'm still here. Disappointed?"

"Never," almost cultishly earnest. I then brought myself back to the present. "You just keep those eyes closed."

"You got a present for me, Mailman?"

"I've got a lot of presents for you. At least one you can unwrap." I said this as I finished placing the candles on the cake and began to light them. 23. An odd number to be in a box. Had Lydia been 23 in the Before?

I walked over holding the cake in front of me, the flickering candles shedding a pale light in the increasing dusk. "Open them."

She did and sat up, then clapped her hands like a child. "I love it! A real birthday cake!"

I then sang "Happy Birthday" to her. When I finished, she cocked her head. "Good thing you're cute, Mailman, because you can't sing a lick."

I smiled. "On the contrary. I'm the greatest male vocalist in the world! Besides, you aren't exactly the pop sensation yourself Monotone Diva."

"That's a depressing thought. Couldn't I have been trapped in the afterlife with Frank Sinatra?"

"Who?"

That look again. "I don't know. But he could sing. Before."

"We're here. Before is another time, if it ever even happened." I looked down at my feet. "I can't think of anyone better to spend my apocalypse with."

She closed her eyes and let the comment wash over her. "You're sweet Mailm---, Donald. And I really do love you, for whatever it's worth here, in whatever time we have left."

"It could be forever..."

She didn't take the bait. "It's going to feel like it if you don't cut that cake. I don't remember what cake tastes like, but I remember wax isn't edible. You're dripping," she said, gesturing to the candles.

"There are 23 candles," I pointed out, thinking she might find it as interesting as I did. "Maybe you were 23. Before?"

The mystery expression was back. That mix of happy, sad, wistful. I couldn't place it. Replaced by exaggerated prim. "A lady doesn't tell her age, Donald. And a gentleman doesn't ask. You have so much to learn about courting." She raised her chin in mock arrogance, though I thought I saw a flicker of emotion she tried to hide.

I divvied the saucers I'd grabbed from my house and we cut the cake. "First for the lady!" I said, handing her a slice half the size of her head.

"How am I going to fit through my door if you make me fat?"

"You aren't. It's my master plan to keep you out here with me."

She stopped, the fork halfway to her mouth, then took the bite and spent more time than necessary chewing. "You know we're going to wake up in our own beds when this is over, right? That part I'm confident of. You want me too fat to get out again?"

I smiled, the first fake one since she stepped outside. I didn't like to think about the morning. "No worries. I'll grease your door with gravy from the Hungry Man Pot Roast and pull you right out!"

She made a face, then took another bite of cake. "Ew. I don't even like to think about that," she said around a mouth full of cake.

"Didn't your mama teach you it's not polite to talk with your mouth full?"

"Probably. But I think she also told me to save myself for marriage. You got a ring inside one of those pockets, mailman? I'd like to see you on one knee before me."

"Nope. I guess I could poke a hole in one of my bicycle cards...."

"No... No. Let's not get caught up in whatever societal bullshit happened before." She moved the cake and basket off the blanket, lay down and patted beside her. "C'mere and love me, Donald."

# Twelve: They Made Love in Their Dreams

I'd write about it later in my journal, but I had the decency to blush while doing it and I'm certainly not going into detail here. Just suffice it to say it was as good as I hoped, both of us vocalizing our love, our lust, like we were never going to get another chance. Maybe we weren't.

I rolled off her panting. "Wow. The pelvis between those sexy hipbones is worth epic poems, lady" I said, gazing at her naked form with the hunger of a wolf."

"Your pelvis ain't so bad yourself, bud. Now get over here and snuggle me. It's the gentlemanly thing to do, you know."

It was full dark now, something I rarely saw here. Usually by dark I was inside, writing, reading, eating TV dinners.

"What now, birthday girl?"

She sighed. "Now we make it last as long as we can. Let's just lay here and stare at the stars. I haven't seen the sky since..." her voice became sad. "...since ever."

"We lay in each other's arms looking at the stars. "I'm glad I got to watch the sky with you for the first time, Lydia of the no last name."

"I'm glad I got to meet you, Donald T. Mailman."

I raised on one elbow. "What is the T for?"

"The."

I barked a surprised laugh. "Seriously? My name is Donald The Mailman?"

"You got a birth certificate to prove otherwise?"

"Not a one, Lydia Pretty Pelvis."

She didn't even hit me then. Just lay looking up. "Even if we only get one night..."

"Please don't say that."

She gave me a hard stare. The first I'd seen since getting to see her eyes. "I'm not going to hide from it, Donald. That would risk me wasting the time I know we have."

"I'll come find you again. We'll do it all over."

She looked sad. "Maybe. I hope...." she began to cry

softly. "I hope I'm there in 320 Sycamore. I hope you're there in your house."

"I will be..."

"Remember, Donald. Reality. We're not going to sully this with pretty lies."

She stopped and just stared at the stars for a few minutes. I tried think of something to say.

Then quiet. "I love you, Donald. I hope I'll love you tomorrow. I *will* love you tomorrow, no matter what happens to either of us. Whatever comes next."

"Me too. However long this lasts, that isn't going to change."

"Put that in your journal, if you can. Just in case." I swore I would. I knew I would.

She put on a brave smile. "Good. I deserve it after giving you my purity..."

I snorted.

"After handing you my maidenhead for a slice of cake, Donald T Uncouth Mailman." Serious again. "Now come over here and give me some of that one more time before sleep."

I did. It was better the second time, hard as that is to believe. After, we lay once again panting arms and legs tangled.

"I loved you, Donald." Her voice sounded sleepy and I, alarmed, felt the drowsiness taking me too, though I couldn't stop it. "I'm glad I knew you." she mumbled, sleep starting to take her.

"I *love* you. I'm glad I *know* you. Present tense. Always present tense."

She nodded and mumbled, then her breathing became the steady breath of sleep.

I felt sleep taking me too. I stopped struggling. I kissed her now sleeping lips one more time, then each closed eyelid.

I fell into the dreamless nothing I had come to expect from this place.

I woke in my bed. I knew better but still looked over hoping to see Lydia beside me, our little domestic '50s life beginning (though part of my vague memories from Before told me an interracial marriage in a town like this in the '50s would have not been welcome). The bed was as empty as it always was. The mail bag was hanging on its hook like always. I went to the refrigerator and found all was normal. A freezer full of Hungry Man Pot Roast.

Except one slice of birthday cake on a plate. I smiled. It happened...

I wanted to run straight to her but I grabbed my journal. Memory was weird here and, even seeing her again and hopefully repeating it, I wanted to capture this experience. I had promised. I wrote in a fever and when I finished my hand hurt and eight pages of the never-ending journal were filled.

I walked out my door to my bicycle, unencumbered. Fuck the mail. I'd deliver it later. I didn't think Lydia would want to go with me, not for that, but I could leave her in the park while I went about my work and come back to her.

I rode as fast as my fixie would fly to 320 Sycamore and ran up to the door, knocking. "Lydia? Lydia? Are you awake? Can you hear me in there? Lydia?"

Silence. A gnawing twist in my stomach.

"Lydia! Lydia?! Come to the door! I want to... I need to hear your voice."

Sobbing from the other side. Not the sad sobbing I'd heard from her before but panicked sobbing. Fear sobbing. "Go away!" she said, the panic in her voice. "Go away, devil! Why are you knocking? Go! Deliver your mail and go! Why are you torturing me?!" Her voice got higher with each sentence.

"Lydia? What are you doing? Lyd----"

"Stop!" Even more rising panic. "I don't know any Lydia! You have the wrong house. Go away." Pleading, scared. "Please. Oh, God, please."

I felt the tears on my face, but couldn't feel the sadness for the profound gut punch delivered to my soul. "You've forgotten me..."

"I haven't forgotten anything! I know you. I know you bring that... that *fucking* mail every day! That horrible, horrible, terrible mail! Why do you bring that mail? What have I done to anger you, God? Go away!"

I started to turn, then remembered the slice of cake in the refrigerator. "Remember the cake?" I shouted. "Did you have cake today? Was our cake in your fridge?"

Screaming. Horrible, piercing, purely terrified screaming. "Oh God. The cake! I ate the cake I didn't even think and the devil brought the cake and I ate it and now I'm doomed I'm going to die I'm going to burn..." All of this in a rush, a babble. Insanity.

I did the only thing I could do. I spared her the fear. I went home, and got the mail. When I got to 320 Sycamore I shoved the mail through the slot silently, but thought I heard her sobbing beside the door. Our usual spot for the book club.

How could she have forgotten me so quickly? That wasn't how memory worked here. You forgot things slowly. You *remembered* you forgot them for a time before it was permanently gone. This panic, this instant reset. This was something else.

As I pedaled it struck me, all of it, and I stopped dead, getting off my bicycle and sitting down in the road. Too stunned to ride.

This was nothing like before, like our first meeting. There was sadness, but not panic. Steel instead of insanity. Fondness? Yes. I remember that. I remember being puzzled by it.

"Lotta ways to hurt, Mailman," I muttered, parroting the words she said to me. Part of her ongoing conviction that us meeting would end badly, that we shouldn't do it. That it was all a mistake. The steely refusal to accept me. The near panic at the thought of me coming into her house; Of her coming into mine. "You'll forget me, mailman. Or I'll forget you... Write me in your journal."

That brought up the whispered phrase. Early. The one I didn't quite catch. The one about my journal. "...different."

Then I knew for sure. This had all happened before, and I'd been the one who forgot. This time. Maybe last time I went into her house instead of her coming outside. Maybe we both went into my house. Maybe we did something completely different or nothing at all. Maybe which of us forgot was random. 23 candles on the cake. 23 meetings? Surely not so many. Surely...

But we *had* met. She knew what meeting me meant.

She knew a face to face would end with one of us forgetting.

And she made sure it was her.

"Oh... Lydia..."

I lay down in the road then. It was the bravest act I could conceive. She sacrificed it all, her memory, all her memories, the warmth of that night... Because she knew I'd remember. She wanted me to remember this time. To write in my journal. To give this... whatever this was supposed to be, some permanence.

I don't remember delivering the rest of the mail. I don't remember going home. I don't remember eating my Hungry Man Dinner. My first memory is eating the cake (this with a twinge of guilt, but knowing eating my last piece of her was less awful than watching it slowly rot in the refrigerator). I sat up and wrote in my journal. Wrote it all. Read over my notes from the night before and made new ones. Wrote about the cake, about the forgetting, about the sacrifice, about the pain.

Then I went to sleep. Truly, fully alone for the first time since I arrived here. You aren't really alone when you're all the world contains. You're just you. But when you know there are others and you can't see them. That's truly alone.

I woke feeling no better. The plate that held the cake now clean and put away, as it always was. Maybe there was a Cosmic Housekeeper too, I thought, without humor.

And, of course, the mailbag on the hook. Whatever my pain, whatever my new reality, I never got a day off. The mail was eternal.

I slowly sorted it, dreading when I made it to Sycamore but determined not to move it to the back. I had to deliver there from now to eternity. Besides, I thought, we'd met at least twice (twenty-three times?) now. I'd have to take it slow but I now knew with absolute certainty that we'd meet again. Eventually. 24 candles on a cake, maybe.

When I did get to Sycamore in my sorting, I frowned. I'd delivered the mail so many times I knew exactly how a bundle felt in my hands. This one was fatter, heavier. I flipped through the mail until I got to an envelope larger than normal. Still slim enough to fit a letterbox, but bulky. I knew better than to open it and didn't have to anyway. I could feel the familiar shape of a book, of a pencil. And I knew exactly what it was. I was delivering Lydia a journal.

I looked over reflexively to ensure I wasn't delivering *my* journal, but seeing it resting in its spot on the nightstand. I felt intense gratitude to Lydia for not letting me give it to her. It wasn't my connection to Before at all.

It was my connection to Lydia. Insurance against me being the one to forget next time, or at least having a record of what I forgot.

Now I was delivering Lydia her own insurance.

I finished sorting the mail and buckled the mailbag onto my bike. I delivered the mail taking my usual route. I said nothing as I walked up to 320 Sycamore, not wanting to scare her. I had all the time in the world, and this had to be taken slow.

As I walked away, I whispered "write me, Lydia the Nameless. Write me this time and remember."

I rode on, hoping I had the courage she did, to ensure I was the one who forgot next time, trusting in my journal to bring me back, at least partially, letting her fill hers for the next time. Or the next. Or the next. 30 candles. 40. A whole bonfire if necessary. As many as it took.

This place wasn't Hell. It wasn't Heaven. It wasn't an Apocalypse or some Biblical Purgatory.

This place was a spiral, shifting slightly each time so the lines never met but ran concentrically. Except now I sensed they might get closer instead of farther apart. Until they intersected.

As dusk fell, I rode toward home, ready to start the first day of the rest of my Afterlife. Of *this* Afterlife.

# Acknowledgments

A novella might not seem like such a big deal to most. Not when there are people writing eight volume, thousand page series every day. But it was a big deal to *me*. While I'd written a lot of short stories, this was my first novella, and it scared the shit out of me. A lot of people, past and present, got me through my "this is too much for me to handle" doubts.

First, and always most important, my wife Joan. She's my biggest cheerleader, my first beta reader, the person who patiently stopped whatever she was doing to read partial chapters that I was stressed to finish. She put up with a writer's moods, entire evenings alone as ideas seized me and were put down before forgotten. Surliness when the words wouldn't come. Babbling about plot points in the middle of TV shows. She's my Lydia. And, if I'm lucky, she always will be.

Thanks to Tony Hays. Tony was my first creative writing teacher in college and the person who gave my so much insight into the confusing feelings I experienced. He is the one who taught me that you don't create your book. Your characters already know what they want to do. Your job is to lose your ego and listen to them. I lost touch with Tony as my fiction muse took a decade-long holiday. When I sought him out to thank him, I found he had died. I lost a lot of years of good advice from embarrassment at being unable to use the gifts he gave. If you're looking for some great reads, Tony's books are the ticket.

To John Prine. The lyrics to "Donald and Lydia" are his and as soon as I started thinking of names for my characters I knew it had to be. I'd like to think if there's an afterlife John's lyrics would be one of the things I remember. At dark times in my life, they were the only words that mattered.

To Matthew "Doc" Kemp, my first non-wife beta reader and a friend for more years than either of us care to remember. Thanks, Doc. This would be a very different, and worse, book without your sage advice.

To Kelly Lapczynski, my Once and Future Editor, who for almost three decades has patiently endured my splicing commas like a serial killer. And being the best friend a fellow could have.

A huge shout out to the members of my Patreon. While I'm never going to retire on the money I make there, the simple fact of having people willing to give you money to write things is a salve against self-doubt that sustained me more than once. They saw *Hell is for Mailmen* first and they gave me the guts to put it out there for public consumption.

And, finally, you. I always hesitate to call my work "art" as it feels pretentious, but art in general is in peril, throttled by a world that increasingly feels entitled to consume it for free. Whatever led you to lay money down to read this, means you love art enough to feel it has value. You are an endangered species, and a beautiful one.

Made in the USA
Coppell, TX
21 May 2022

78030947R00033